Hi Bears,
Bye Bears

by Niki Yektai
illustrated by Diane deGroat

Orchard Books   New York

The illustrator wishes to thank her model, Elan, for being a good bear-hugger.

Orchard Books, A division of Franklin Watts, Inc.
387 Park Avenue South, New York, NY 10016

Manufactured in the United States of America
Printed by General Offset Co., Inc. Bound by Horowitz/Rae. Book design by Mina Greenstein. The text of this book is set in 24 pt. ITC Garamond Book. The illustrations are watercolors, reproduced in full color.

10 9 8 7 6 5 4 3 2 1

Library of Congress Cataloging-in-Publication Data
Yektai, Niki. Hi bears, bye bears / by Niki Yektai ; illustrated by Diane deGroat.   p.   cm.
Summary: A child chooses from among a group of teddy bears.
ISBN 0-531-05858-1. ISBN 0-531-08458-2 (lib. bdg.)
[1. Teddy bears—Fiction. 2. Stories in rhyme.]   I. deGroat, Diane, ill.   II. Title.   PZ8.3.Y43Hi
1991   89-37554   CIP   AC   [E]—dc20.

BOMC offers recordings and compact discs, cassettes and records. For information and catalog write to BOMR, Camp Hill, PA 17012.

For my uncle,
Michael E. Kulukundis

N.Y.

Two bears

Four bears

Here come more bears.

Groom bear   Bride bear

Slim bear

Wide bear

Soft bear

Rich bear

Poor bear

Witch bear

Mom bear   Dad bear

Good bear

Bad bear

Weak bear

Strong bear

Short bear

Long bear

Dizzy bear

Frizzy bear

Sleepy bear

Weepy bear

Bear with mail

Bear on toes

Bear with pail

Bear with hose

Bear with bat   Bear with board

Bear with ball   Bear with sword

Bear in blue

Bear in white

Bear with cake   Bear with light

These bears kiss

This bear drinks

These bears hug

This bear stinks

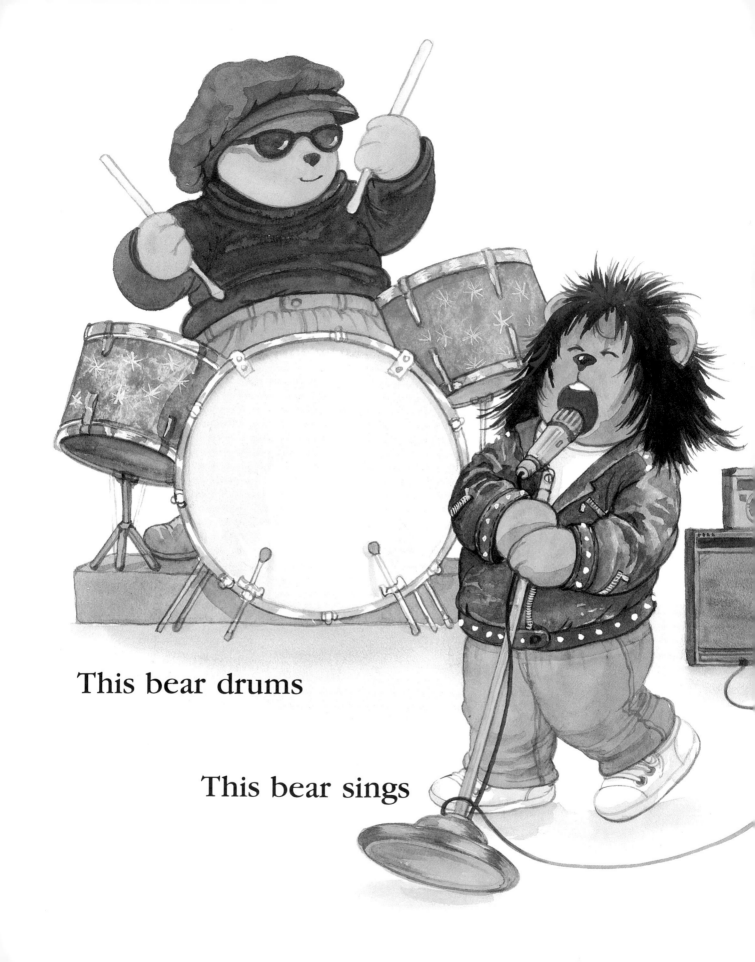

This bear drums

This bear sings

This bear strums

This bear swings

Hurry, bears!

Sam is coming!

Which one will he choose?
He loves them all.
But he can have only one.

He chooses Soft bear.
Which bear would you choose?